Book 1

Shelter Pet Squad

Jelly Bean

by
CYNTHIA LORD

illustrated by
ERIN MCGUIRE

Scholastic Inc.

To Mona

ISBN 978-0-545-63597-4

10 9 8 7 6 5 4 3 2 1   14 15 16 17 18 19/0
Printed in the U.S.A.   23
First edition, September 2014

The text type was set in Janson MT.
Book design by Nina Goffi

Chapter 1

Even If It's Not Perfect

Dad calls my bedroom "Suzannah's Pet Shop," because stuffed animals have taken over! They play hide-and-seek between the books on my shelf. They bounce with me when I jump on my bed. They snuggle against my neck and beg for treats.

It's fun pretending with my stuffed animals, but I wish I could have a *real* pet. Something soft and furry that could sit in the window, waiting

for the school bus to bring me home. My pet would bound across the living room to greet me. He'd jump into my lap before I even sat down.

If I couldn't have a big pet, I'd pick something little and busy. He could live in a cage in my room. I'd build him a fun playground with paper-towel-tube tunnels to scurry through and ramps to climb up and slide down. My pet would ride in my bathrobe pocket when I made breakfast: cereal for me, carrots for him.

But the only pets I can have are stuffed animals. We live in an apartment, and the landlord says:

No dogs.

No cats.

No pets of any kind.

Only *people* can live in our apartment.

I don't think that's fair. A fish wouldn't make a mess. A lizard isn't noisy. A hamster doesn't smell bad — well, not too bad.

"Maybe someday we'll have our own house," Mom says. "And then we can make the rules. But right now, this apartment is a good home for us. Even if it's not perfect."

Sometimes I put my stuffed-animal dog, Bentley, in the window to watch me come home from school. I carry Whiskers, my stuffed-animal mouse, in my bathrobe pocket while I make breakfast. Mom bought me a collar with a bell so that Oscar, my stuffed cat, doesn't surprise Tweets, my toy bird.

"Pretending is fun, but it's not the same as *really* doing something," I told Mom.

One day I was lining up my stuffed animals to watch TV with me. "Suzannah," Mom said, "I have an idea. I just read about a new program for kids to help at the animal shelter. I thought you might like to go."

"What's an animal shelter?" I asked.

"The shelter is a place for stray animals and homeless pets. The people who work there take care of the animals and try to find homes for them," Mom explained. "The new program is called Shelter Pet Squad. Kids from second through sixth grade can sign up to come in on Saturday mornings. They will help make toys and do special things for the animals. I think you might like it, Suzannah. Want to give it a try?"

"It wouldn't be like having my own pet," I said slowly.

"No, it wouldn't be the same," Mom said. "But it still might be fun."

"What kinds of animals do they have at a shelter?" I asked.

"Mostly dogs and cats," Mom said. "But some other animals, too."

The shelter animals didn't have a home — not yet. And I couldn't have a real pet — not yet. But maybe we could borrow each other? Even if it was just for now and not "for keeps"?

Even if it wasn't perfect.

"Okay," I said. "I'll try it."

Little Things Matter

On Saturday, Mom drove me to the animal shelter. I felt tingly with excitement. I couldn't wait to see the animals and make things for them.

But I was a little bit worried, too. Second grade was the bottom age for Shelter Pet Squad. Would there be any other second graders, like me?

And I'd never had a pet before. What if I

didn't know what to do? What if the animals didn't like me?

I really wanted them to like me.

Before we left home, I hid my stuffed-animal mouse in my pocket. Whiskers is a brave mouse, and he makes me feel brave, too.

"We're here!" Mom parked in front of a big red building. A sign out front said MAPLEWOOD ANIMAL SHELTER. I reached into my pocket and touched Whiskers's nose. His nose is his bravest part, because it leads him into adventures.

Inside the shelter, there was a waiting room with shiny floors. There were racks of colorful leashes and collars, silver pet dishes, and cushy dog beds for sale. Behind the cash register were filing cabinets, bookcases, and a bulletin board covered with photos of animals. A striped orange cat walked across the counter. A gray cat was curled up asleep in one of the chairs.

"Hello!" said the lady behind the counter. She lifted the orange cat out of the way. "Can I help you?"

"This is Suzannah." Mom put her hand on my shoulder. "She's here for Shelter Pet Squad."

"How nice to meet you, Suzannah! I'm Ms. Flores. Thank you for helping our animals. Ms. Kim is in charge of Shelter Pet Squad. She's in the workroom with the rest of the kids. Just go right through that door and you'll find them."

Mom opened the door to the workroom. I saw four kids and one adult sitting around a table with markers and paper bags and a big bowl of dog biscuits. I didn't know anyone. All the kids looked older than me.

"Hello. I'm Ms. Kim," the woman said, smiling. "You must be Suzannah. Come in. You're just in time!"

I slipped my hand into my pocket to touch Whiskers' nose. I knew *he* wasn't feeling scared.

"This looks fun," Mom said. "Do you want me to stay, Suzannah? Or are you okay by yourself?"

No other parents were there. "I'm okay," I said quietly.

"Dad will pick you up in an hour," Mom said. "Have fun!"

I opened my mouth to say good-bye, but the word got stuck on the way out. So I just nodded.

"I have a name tag for you to wear around your neck," Ms. Kim said. "May I put it on you?"

I nodded again. It went over my head like a necklace, with a plastic name card at the bottom. Under my name, it said SHELTER PET SQUAD

MEMBER. I glanced at the other kids around the table: Levi, Jada, Matt, and a girl whose long black hair covered up her name tag. In my head, I called her Pink Girl because everything she wore was pink — even her shoes. Jada and Pink Girl looked like third or fourth graders, but Levi and Matt were probably fifth or sixth graders.

"When the dogs are in their cages, they need things to do," Ms. Kim said. "So today we're putting dog biscuits in paper bags. Then we will scrunch each bag into the shape of a ball. The dog will smell the treats inside and will work to get them out. So it's like a puzzle. Some dogs will figure it out really fast. For other dogs, it will take some time. We're going to make one for every dog at the shelter. It's a little thing we can do for them, but little things matter."

Ms. Kim showed us a whiteboard where she had written a list of the dogs' names.

Bandit, 2
Gordie, 3
Patches, 3
Brutus, 3
Sweetie, 2
Abby, 3
Dusty, 3
Toby, 3
Max, 2
Bella, 3
Sunny, 3
Coco, 2
Texas, 3

"The number is how many treats for that dog," Ms. Kim said. "We don't want the dogs to gain too much weight while they're with us. So two treats for the little dogs and three treats for the big dogs."

That didn't seem too hard. I chose an empty chair between Levi and Pink Girl. I took a red marker and a bag from the pile in the middle of the table.

"Suzannah, you can make bags for Bandit and Sunny. Write the dog's name near the bottom of the bag. Then put the correct number of treats inside and scrunch. Levi can show you."

Levi had dark, curly hair and a friendly smile. "I made a ball for Brutus." He showed me his scrunched-up paper-bag ball. "Ms. Kim, when we're done, can we give these to our dogs and watch them open them?"

"Yes, of course!" Ms. Kim said. "This is the work part. That will be the fun part."

Even the work part seemed pretty fun to me. I wrote in my best letters *B-A-N-D-I-T* on the bottom of the bag. The marker squeaked as I wrote.

"Bandit sounds like Band-Aid!" Pink Girl said.

I looked at the word on my bag. Did I spell it wrong? No. It said *Bandit*, just like Ms. Kim had written it on the board. I wasn't sure if Pink Girl was joking or making fun of my dog.

"It's Bandit," I said firmly. I slid my bag closer to Levi and away from her.

"Bandit must be a little dog, because he only gets two biscuits," Levi said. "Both of my dogs are big, because they each get three." He grinned. "My dog at home is named Penny. She would get *four* biscuits! She's a sheepdog and she's huge."

"I have a pet rabbit at home," Jada said. "His name is Honeybun."

Matt laughed. "Honeybun?"

Jada shrugged. "My little sister named him. He likes me best, though. I bring him carrots and lettuce."

"I have two cats and a hamster," Matt said.

"I want a dog, but my dad doesn't think our cats would like it. Someday I want to have a golden retriever. My aunt has one named Ben."

"My dog is the best dog in the whole wide world," Pink Girl said. "My grandpa calls him a dust mop. He's really a Yorkshire terrier. His name is Ringo, and we have to take him to the groomer or else his hair just grows and grows."

Everyone looked at me, as if it was my turn. I didn't want to be the only one without a pet. "I have a mouse named Whiskers," I said.

No one said the pets had to be real.

"Cool," Jada said. "I wish I had a mouse."

"I don't have any pets at home," Ms. Kim said. "My husband has allergies. So the animals at the shelter are my pets while they're here."

Ms. Kim didn't have a real pet of her own, either? It made me feel better to know I wasn't the only one. I smiled and picked a green dog biscuit and a yellow dog biscuit out of the bowl

for Bandit. I hoped he'd like having two flavors, not just one.

"Now for the scrunching!" Levi said to me. "Just pretend you're making a snowball."

I pushed and squished and squashed. It was a messy-looking ball, but I hoped Bandit would think it was fun.

For Sunny, I picked a yellow marker and wrote *S-U-N-N-Y* on the bag. I drew a big sun at the end.

"Sunny is sunny in two ways," Ms. Kim told me. "She's yellow like the sun, and she's bouncy and happy. So she makes everyone around her feel sunny *inside.*"

I gave Sunny three treats: green, yellow,

and red. I squished the bag tight. I wanted her to have lots of fun getting it open.

When we had a pile of paper-bag balls, Ms. Kim said, "Okay, Shelter Pet Squad. Are you ready to meet the dogs?"

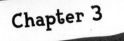

Chapter 3

The Kennel

On the way to the dog kennel, Ms. Kim gave us a tour of the animal shelter. First we peeked into the small-animal room. There were only empty cages. "Our last rabbit went to her new home yesterday," Ms. Kim said proudly. "But sometimes we have hamsters, gerbils, rats, ferrets, guinea pigs, birds, and rabbits. Once, we even had a pair of chinchillas!"

22

I squeezed the paper-bag balls I had made for my dogs, Bandit and Sunny. When it was time to give them the treats, I hoped Ms. Kim wouldn't pick me to go first. I wasn't sure what to do.

In the hallway, we passed a kitchen and a laundry room and then a room of cats. Some of the cats were lying on the windowsills. Some were curled up on blankets on the floor. Others climbed on towers with platforms to sit on. So many cats! I wished I could go inside the room with them, but Ms. Kim was already opening a big door at the end of the hallway. I hurried to catch up.

The dog kennel had two long rows of big cages. A few of them were empty, but most had a dog inside. There were big dogs, little dogs, black dogs, brown dogs, spotted dogs, and yellow dogs. On each cage was a sign with the dog's name and information on it.

Some of the dogs barked at us. Others came to the edge of the cage, wagging their tails. Ms. Kim stopped at the first cage. "Hey, Dusty! We have something for you!" She turned to Matt. "When I open the door to the pen, toss your treat in to him."

"Can I go inside and pet him?" Matt asked.

Ms. Kim shook her head. "There will be some pets at the shelter that you can play with. But we always have to think about what's best for each animal. Some of our dogs are scared when they first come here. It's hard for them to be in a strange place with new people and dogs. Other dogs come here needing to learn some manners, like not to jump up on people. So we have to keep you safe and the dogs comfortable. But you can talk to them and watch them play with their treats and know that you've made their day special."

Dusty was a big, shaggy, gray dog. He jumped off his bed and went after his treat ball as soon as Matt threw it on the floor of his cage.

"Hey, Dusty!" Matt said. "Can you smell the treats inside? I picked them just for you."

"Allie, did you make a bag for Sweetie?" Ms. Kim asked.

"Yes," Pink Girl said.

Now I knew Pink Girl's name. It was Allie. But "Pink Girl" was already stuck in my head. Maybe I'd call her both names.

"Here Sweetie-weetie!" Allie Pink Girl said in a really high voice.

Sweetie was a skinny little dog, with long legs and tiny feet. She nosed her ball around her cage before she ripped it open and ate the treats. She seemed like a nice dog.

"Suzannah, do you have treats for Bandit?" Ms. Kim called to me from farther down the row of cages.

Bandit was a little black-and-white dog. He stayed in his bed as Ms. Kim opened the cage door. I looked between the scrunches of my bag balls to find Bandit's name, then threw his ball onto the floor of his cage. Bandit stayed on his bed and stared at it.

"Bandit is shy," Ms. Kim said. "He had an owner who loved him very much. But she was an older lady and she died. He misses her. He might not play with it right now, Suzannah. But he'll come get it when he's ready."

The group moved on to the next dog, but I stayed. I watched Bandit through the pen door.

It wasn't fair that he'd lost his person and his home at the same time. "I made this for you," I said softly to him. "There are yummy treats in the bag."

The little dog climbed slowly out of his bed. He walked over to sniff the bag. Picking it up in his teeth, he carried it back to his bed.

I smiled, but my heart hurt, too. Bandit needed someone to help him feel happy again. I wished that someone could be me. "I'm sorry you're sad," I said quietly. "I hope you get a new family soon."

I pulled Whiskers out of my pocket, just far enough that his nose was poking out. "Be brave, okay?" I said in my squeaky mouse voice. "Adventure is ahead!"

Bandit put his foot on the edge of the bag and ripped it with his teeth. He found the first treat and looked up at me while he crunched it.

"Good boy!" I said.

"Suzannah, Sunny wants her turn now!" Ms. Kim called from somewhere in the kennel.

"Bye, Bandit." I pushed Whiskers back down into my pocket so no one would see him. I left Bandit crunching his second dog biscuit.

Sunny was a big golden retriever. She came right over to me with her fluffy tail wagging. I tossed the bag into the cage and she jumped around, ripping it apart. Sunny wouldn't need a pep talk from Whiskers. Sunny was plenty brave already.

"She's the kind of dog I want," Matt said.

Sunny would take up my whole bed at home. I still wished I could take her home, though. I wouldn't mind sleeping on the floor if we didn't both fit.

"Sunny really likes your treats," Jada said, smiling at me.

I smiled back. Jada looked like she might want to be friends with me. "I gave Sunny one of each flavor."

"That was a good idea," Jada said. "If I could

adopt a dog, Sunny is the dog I'd pick. Which one would you pick?"

"I want to adopt them all!" I said.

Jada laughed. "Then you'd have an animal shelter at your house!"

"The dogs are happy and busy now," said Ms. Kim. "So let's go back to the workroom. I brought some fleece for us to braid into simple rope toys for the cats to pounce on and swat." She grinned at Matt. "And then you can play with the cats."

"Hooray!" Matt said.

As we walked back to the door of the kennel, Ms. Kim spoke to each dog. "You're such a pretty girl, Bella. Hi, Patches. You'll be going for a walk soon. Hey, Max! Who's a good dog?"

I could tell she loved the dogs. But a cage wasn't the same as a house. I wanted the dogs to have homes all their own.

On our way out of the kennel, I walked slowly on purpose. I kept turning around one more time to see Bandit and Sunny. One more time. One more time.

It had been fun making things for the dogs and seeing how much they liked them. But it hurt to walk away. Would they get adopted this week? Would I ever see them again?

I looked back one more time.

Chapter 4

Jelly Bean

At the shelter, there were lots of cats! One little black kitten liked the braided fleece toy I made. She liked it so much that no other cats got to play with it! I dragged it along the floor and she pounced on it, over and over.

I would've stayed there all day. But after a while, Ms. Kim said it was time to clean up the workroom and meet our parents in the waiting room. In the workroom, Levi put the leftover dog biscuits back in the box. Matt cleaned up the fleece scraps. Jada and I put the markers and extra paper bags in the cupboards. Allie Pink Girl and Ms. Kim used wet sponges to wash the table. "Thank you," Ms. Kim said. "I'll see you all next week."

"That was really fun!" said Allie Pink Girl. "I loved the cats!"

All the other kids' parents were in the waiting room. Jada waved to me as she left with her mom and little sister. My dad was nowhere in sight.

"I can't wait for next Saturday," Levi said, leaving with his parents.

"I'm sure your dad will be here soon, Suzannah," Ms. Kim said. "I need to walk the dogs, but you can stay here with Ms. Flores and play with our waiting-room cats. If your dad doesn't come in a few minutes, we'll call your mom in case he forgot. How does that sound?"

I smiled. I'd get to play with these cats all by myself! "Good!" It seemed like a long time ago that I felt nervous to be there.

Ms. Flores, behind the front counter, told me the orange cat was named Hattie. "And the gray cat is Shadow. They both love to greet our visitors."

Sitting next to Shadow, I ran my hand down her side. She was so soft. Then she purred! A rumbly, happy purr. "Ms. Flores, can I go to the cat room and get one of the toys we made?" I asked. "I think Shadow might like to play with one."

"Of course!" she said.

It was exciting to walk down the hall to the cat room all by myself, wearing my name tag. I was an official Shelter Pet Squad member on a mission! As I walked into the cat room, some of the cats meowed or flicked their tails. One pretty orange tiger cat rubbed her face against my leg. The black kitten I had played with was curled up, fast asleep next to the cat toy I had made.

I picked up another braided toy. "I'll be back next week," I promised.

Back in the waiting room, I held one end of the toy. I dangled the other end over Shadow's head. She grabbed it with her front paws, attacking it.

The bell above the front door rang. I was having so much fun with Shadow that I was glad it wasn't Dad. A family brought in a huge bag of dog food. "We wanted to give this to the shelter," the mom told Ms. Flores.

"Oh, thank you! We'd be glad to have it," Ms. Flores said.

Next a veterinarian stopped by. "How's Abby doing on that new medicine?" he asked Ms. Flores.

"She is much better!" Ms. Flores said.

"That's great," he said. "I'm going down to the kennel to have a look at her."

"You're a beautiful cat," I whispered to Shadow as the front door opened again.

I looked up to see if it was Dad. No, it was a family. There was a mom and dad, each holding one end of a big cage. A girl about my age walked behind them. She was crying.

I know it's not nice to stare, but I couldn't stop. I let Shadow pull the cat toy from my fingers.

"Hello," the mom said to Ms. Flores. "My husband just accepted a job in France, and we're moving next week. Our guinea pig isn't allowed to come with us. We have no one to take him. We were hoping you'd find him a new home."

"Yes, of course," Ms. Flores said kindly. "I'll just need you to fill out some forms."

The mom and dad set the cage down on the floor so they could write on the papers.

"His name is Jelly Bean," the girl told Ms. Flores, sniffling. "He's a great guinea pig."

I sat up taller so I could see down into the cage. A brown-and-white guinea pig face peeked out of a little wooden house inside.

"Are you leaving his cage and little house and dishes, too?" Ms. Flores asked.

"Yes," the dad said. "You may have everything."

"Thank you," said Ms. Flores. "Jelly Bean

will be more comfortable with some familiar things. And it's easier to find someone to adopt the small pets if they come with a cage." She looked over the forms. "I'm glad to see that he is in good health and he has never bitten anyone. He looks like a wonderful pet."

"He's been a perfect pet," the mom said. "We're sorry that he can't come with us."

"We have a special room for the smaller pets," Ms. Flores said. "If you'll bring him and follow me, I'll show you."

The mom and dad picked up the cage again. The girl covered her face with her hands. I watched her shoulders go up and down as she cried.

I know it's hard not having a pet, but it must

be even worse to give away a pet you already love. Ms. Flores held the door open to the small-animal room.

"It'll be okay," I said to the girl.

She glanced through her fingers at me.

"The people here are nice," I said. "They'll take good care of him."

"He's never lived anywhere else. He'll be sad without me," she said. "And I'll be sad without him."

"I'll be coming here on Saturdays for Shelter Pet Squad." I showed her my name tag. "So I can check on him. I'll make sure he gets a good home."

"Promise?" she asked.

"I promise."

The bell over the front door to the shelter jingled. "I'm sorry I'm late, sweetie," Dad said. "I got lost trying to find the shelter. Are you ready?"

I glanced toward the small-animal room. The girl had gone inside. She was holding Jelly Bean in her arms, saying good-bye.

I nodded to Dad, feeling braver than when I had arrived. I had a *real* mission now. "I'm ready."

Ready to find a new home for Jelly Bean.

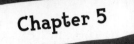

Chapter 5

Trying

On Monday, I woke up excited to find a new home for Jelly Bean. He was such a cute guinea pig. How hard could it be?

Our mail carrier was coming up the side-walk as I left for school. "Mrs. Fisher, how would you like to have a pet guinea pig?" I asked. "He even comes with a cage!"

"Oh, no, thank you!" she said, making a face. "Cleaning cages is too much work. My daughter had a pet rabbit years ago. I was always cleaning the cage."

I didn't even get to tell her how cute Jelly Bean was.

When my bus came, I tried again. Climbing the steps, I said, "Mrs. Scott, do you like guinea pigs? There's a really cute guinea pig at the animal shelter. He needs a new —"

"I have three cats!" my bus driver said. "A guinea pig would be scared to death at my house!"

At school, I saw my principal in the hallway. "Would your kids like a pet guinea pig, Mr. Viera?" I asked. "I know the perfect one."

"My kids have their hearts set on a dog," Mr. Viera said. "I'm just not ready to train a puppy. We're too busy right now."

It was hard to keep hearing no. But it would only take one person saying yes to keep my promise. So I kept trying.

"I have the same problem you do," my

teacher, Mrs. Cole, said. "My landlord says no pets."

The janitor's son was allergic to hay.

The nurse's daughter was allergic to fur.

Every kid I asked wanted Jelly Bean. The next day, I found out that all their parents didn't.

"Sorry. My mom says they're too smelly."

"We don't have a good place to put a big cage."

"I begged, but Dad says we already have too many pets."

"My mom thinks I'm not responsible enough. I told her I was, but she thought we should try a fish first."

"My grandma doesn't like rodents!"

With every no, my stomach felt heavier. By Friday, I had asked everyone I could think of who might adopt Jelly Bean. No one had said yes.

At home, I kept pretending Jelly Bean lived with us. I would put his cage right near the TV so he could watch the news with Dad. Mom would bring him a carrot as she was cooking supper. I would make fun play areas for him in my room. Jelly Bean was used to having a family, and that's what he needed again.

But I couldn't adopt him either.

"Don't worry," Dad said at suppertime. "It'll happen."

"Maybe when you get to Shelter Pet Squad tomorrow, you'll find out that Jelly Bean has already been adopted," Mom added. "You aren't the only person trying to find him a home. Ms. Kim and Ms. Flores are trying, too. I'm sure they've told every visitor to the shelter about Jelly Bean. Maybe one of them adopted him."

I nodded, but that idea only made me half happy. "I wanted someone I *know* to adopt him. Then I could ask about him sometimes. I could find out if he was happy in his new home."

Still, I crossed my fingers that Mom was right. I hoped he'd already been adopted by a family that would love him.

And didn't mind cleaning cages.

And lived in a place where pets were allowed.

And didn't have allergies.

And didn't have cats that didn't like guinea pigs.

I sighed. Finding Jelly Bean a good home was much harder than I'd thought it would be.

Chapter 6

Finding a Good Match

On Saturday, I wasn't scared to go back to the shelter. But I still put Whiskers in my pocket, just in case.

Ms. Kim met us as soon as we came through the waiting room door. Before I could even ask her about Jelly Bean, she said, "Ms. Flores has something special to show us!"

Jada grinned at me. I walked over to stand

next to her. I was glad to be making a new friend.

"Look over here." Ms. Flores pointed to the bulletin board on the wall behind the front desk. "This is where we post photos of the animals that have been adopted. As they leave the shelter, we take their picture. Sometimes the families even send us photos of their pets in their new homes. Seeing our animals happy and loved by their new families makes all our hard work worth it."

The bulletin board had lots of photos. There were people holding cats or kneeling beside dogs with the Maplewood Animal Shelter sign in the background. I looked quickly across the photos. Where was —?

"Suzannah, look!" Ms. Kim said.

Jelly Bean? I hurried over to the picture Ms. Flores was pointing to.

"It's Bandit!" Ms. Kim said.

Oh. Well, that was good news, too! In the photo, a lady was kneeling next to Bandit, holding his leash. She was smiling, but Bandit looked nervous.

It'll be okay, I wanted to tell him. *Just wait and see. It's scary to meet new people, but it won't be scary forever, only at first.* There wasn't a photo of him at his new house. So I imagined him happily playing with some dog toys on the couch next to the lady.

"There's Brutus!" Levi said. "I'm glad he has a new home!" I looked at the other photos of pets and their new families. I recognized some of the dogs, but I didn't see Sunny.

"What about Sunny?" I asked. "And Jelly Bean?"

"Not yet," Ms. Flores said. "Sunny has lots of energy. She'll need a yard with room to run. And no one has come to the shelter wanting a guinea pig. Most people are looking for a dog or a cat."

As the other kids talked about the photos, I walked over to the doorway to the small-animal room. Jelly Bean saw me right away. *"Wheeek!"* He ran to the side of his cage. Standing up on his hind legs, he held the cage bars with his tiny paws. *"Wheeek!"*

He looked so cute. I wished I could pick him up and hold him. *"Wheeek!"*

"That means 'I want a treat!'" Ms. Flores said, coming up beside me. "There are some carrots under his cage, Suzannah. Would you like to give him one?"

I was excited to give Jelly Bean a treat. As I came closer, he turned his face to the side to see what I was doing. I pulled a carrot out of the bag.

"Wheeek!"

"Who's this?" Matt asked.

I turned around to see everyone had followed me into the small-animal room.

"His name is Jelly Bean." I felt proud that I could introduce him to the other kids because I had met him first.

Levi smiled. "Jelly Bean is a funny name for a guinea pig."

"He's *shaped* like a jelly bean," Matt said. "Maybe that's why they named him Jelly Bean."

I pushed the end of the carrot through the bars. Jelly Bean grabbed it with his teeth and pulled it the rest of the way inside. He started chomping and chewing.

"He sure likes carrots!" Jada said. "Just like my rabbit, Honeybun!"

"He'll make someone a great pet," Ms. Flores said. "We just need to find the right person."

"Jelly Bean has his treat now," Ms. Kim said. "Are you ready to make some treats for the dogs?"

"Yes!" everyone said.

"Great!" Ms. Kim said. "Come with me to the workroom."

I walked beside Jada so we could sit together. This time we hid treats in paper-towel tubes. We cut the tubes in half and then folded over an edge at one end to make a little cup. We put a handful of cheese cubes and broken-up dog biscuits in the tube. Then we folded over the other end to seal the treats inside.

"It's like a little package," Jada said.

"Yeah, we're mail carriers delivering treat packages!" Matt said. "Special delivery for Abby!"

"It's like a puzzle for them. The dogs will

smell the cheese and work to get it out of the tube," Ms. Kim said. "It's the same idea as the paper-bag balls we made last week, but with a different problem to solve."

"Isn't it mean to make them work for their treats?" Allie Pink Girl asked.

"Not at all," Ms. Kim said. "Dogs like to be busy and play. This gives them something to do and a treat for doing it."

"Can I make one for Jelly Bean?" I asked.

"Guinea pigs don't eat cheese or dog biscuits, but they *do* like to chew cardboard," Ms. Kim said. "Go ahead and make an extra tube and just fold over one end, Suzannah. When we're done with the dogs, we'll find a good treat to put inside for Jelly Bean."

Allie Pink Girl laughed. "We should give him jelly beans!"

"He likes carrots," I said, sticking my chin up.

"Carrots are a much better idea," Ms. Kim said. "Candy would make him sick. We give our animals only healthy treats."

I liked that my idea was a "much better idea."

"What happens if an animal doesn't get adopted?" Jada asked.

"They live here with us," Ms. Kim said. "If the animal has been here a long time, we might ask another shelter in a different town to take him. Maybe the right family isn't here. Maybe the animal will have a better chance somewhere else. But we do everything we can. We put each animal's photo on our website. We tell all the people who come into the shelter about our pets."

I made the extra treat tube for Jelly Bean. Then I put it off to the side so it wouldn't get mixed in with the dogs' treats.

"But we don't want just *any* home," Ms. Kim continued. "Some animals need special care. Or a family might have other pets, too. Will the animals all get along? There are a lot of things to think about and questions to ask. We need to find a good match for each animal and each family."

"What would be a good match for Jelly Bean?" I asked.

"The right person would give him a safe, clean place to live, healthy food, hay, and fresh water. And he'll need toys or things to keep him busy, and plenty of attention," Ms. Kim said. "Guinea pigs can get lonely. So it would be nice if his cage were placed where he will feel part of the family."

We brought our treat tubes to the dogs in the kennel. I gave mine to Sunny. She had no trouble getting it open! Then I headed to the waiting room with Jelly Bean's empty paper-towel tube. I wanted to ask Ms. Flores if I could have some carrot bits to put inside.

"We have lots of wonderful cats," Ms. Flores was saying to a lady at the counter. "Are you looking for a kitten or an older cat?"

"Or a guinea pig?" I asked. "There's a really nice one in the small-animal room. His name is Jelly Bean and he's really friendly."

The woman squirmed. "I want a cat to get *rid* of rodents."

I stepped backward. She was definitely a bad match for Jelly Bean!

Waiting for Ms. Flores to finish talking to the lady, my heart sank. It had been a whole week. Not one person had been a good match.

I'd promised to help, but what if I couldn't?

What if *no one* wanted a guinea pig?

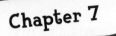

Chapter 7

Operation Jelly Bean

The next week, I was so happy to find Sunny's adoption photo on the bulletin board. In the photo, Sunny was sitting beneath the Maplewood Animal Shelter sign with four kids. Her mouth was partly open as if she was smiling. "She has gone to live with a family that has a big backyard for her to run in," Ms. Kim said. "She'll love that."

"I'm glad she got a good home with lots of kids," Jada said.

Sunny's family had sent a photo of her at her new home, too. Two boys were playing outside, and Sunny was right there with them. Her tail was wagging so fast it was blurry in the photo.

I looked at every other photo on the bulletin board. No Jelly Bean.

"I brought Jelly Bean an apple," I told Ms. Flores and Ms. Kim. "I borrowed a guinea pig book from the library. It said guinea pigs like apples."

"He'll love that," Ms. Flores said. "But let's cut it up. The seeds aren't good for little animals."

Ms. Flores found a small knife and cut my apple into chunks. "These can go in his bowl. Would you like to give them to him, Suzannah?"

I was hoping she'd say that!

Jelly Bean ran to the front of his cage when he saw me.

"Wheeek!"

"I have a special treat for you," I said, opening the cage door. I put the apple chunks in his bowl. He came right up beside my hand, so I stroked his back gently with my finger. I thought he might run into his hidey house, but he didn't. "I hope you like apples," I said.

He liked them so much that he started crunching and munching as soon as I stopped

66

petting him. As I closed the cage door, I heard someone come into the small-animal room behind me. I thought it was one of the other kids, until a man's voice said, "I was told there's a guinea pig in here?"

I turned around. The man was wearing dirty jeans and a black T-shirt. Maybe he was looking for a pet for one of his kids? "Yes, this is Jelly Bean," I said. "He's a wonderful guinea pig."

The man didn't smile. "Do you know how much he costs?"

"He's twenty dollars. The cage is ten."

I was about to tell him that a guinea pig needs attention, but he said, "I don't need the cage. Do you think they'd take five dollars for him?"

"I don't know." I felt my eyebrows come down. I didn't like that he thought Jelly Bean should cost less money. "He's worth twenty dollars."

"Twenty dollars is a lot for snake food," he said.

Snake food! He wanted Jelly Bean so a snake could eat him? This would not be a good match at all! This would be the worst match ever!

"Oh, wait," I said quickly. "Are you talking about *this* guinea pig? I'm sorry. I didn't understand. This guinea pig is not for sale. He's, um, sick."

The man gave me a funny look. "Sick?"

"Yes." I tried to remember the "health" section in the guinea pig book I had borrowed from the library. I couldn't remember any names of real diseases. So I made one up. "This guinea pig has sneezy flu. That's why he's all by himself in here. We don't want any other animals to catch it."

The man bit his lower lip. He looked like he was trying to decide if I was telling the truth.

"It's very catching." I stuck my nose out bravely, just like Whiskers. "Your snake will definitely get sick if he eats him. Some snakes *die* from it."

"Twenty dollars is more than I wanted to pay, anyway." He turned away and left the room.

I breathed out a long breath. *Whew.* That was a close call.

"There you are, Suzannah!" Ms. Kim said as I came out of the small-animal room. Levi, Allie Pink Girl, Jada, and Matt were in the waiting room. "We're ready to get to work," Ms. Kim said. "How's Jelly Bean this morning? Did he like his apple pieces?"

I felt ill — like I had sneezy flu, too. I pointed out the window to the man crossing the parking lot. "I told that man he couldn't adopt Jelly Bean," I said.

"Suzannah!" Ms. Kim said. "Why did you do that? Jelly Bean needs a home."

"That man wasn't going to give him a home," I said. "He wanted Jelly Bean for his snake's lunch!"

"Oh! I'm glad you talked him out of it," Levi said.

"Snakes need to eat, but we don't want one to eat Jelly Bean," Matt said.

Ms. Kim nodded. "I'm sorry, Suzannah. You're right. That would not have been a good match for Jelly Bean."

I stood up taller. I had saved Jelly Bean.

But Ms. Flores smiled sadly. "I do wish the right person would adopt him. I worry he's sad being alone so much. Not all animals do well with noise and different hands holding them, but Jelly Bean likes people. He seems happy when he's in the middle of everything."

"He wouldn't be happy in the middle of a snake, though!" said Jada.

"No, you're right. We'll keep hoping for him," Ms. Kim said. "But now Ms. Flores and I have a special surprise. I need you all to wait right here while we go see if they're ready for us."

I looked down at my sneakers. I had saved Jelly Bean from a bad home, but he still didn't have a good one.

"The waiting room is the right place for waiting!" Allie Pink Girl said, flopping down in one of the chairs. "Maybe the surprise is a new dog?"

"Or maybe it's an animal we don't see very much, like a llama!" Matt said.

"That would *really* be a surprise," Levi said. "Suzannah, are you okay?"

I glanced up. They were all staring at me. My mouth was dry, and I felt like crying. "I'm worried Jelly Bean won't get a home," I said. "And I told his first family I'd find him one."

"You met them?" Jada asked.

"I was here when his family brought him to the shelter. The girl was crying. I promised her —" I stopped because I didn't want to cry, too.

"Don't worry," Levi said. "Lots of people like guinea pigs."

"That's true," Matt said. "My cousin had

one in his preschool. I was really jealous. My teachers only ever bought fish."

"Wouldn't it be great if a teacher took him?" Jada said. "Ms. Flores said he likes to be in the middle of things. There's a lot of action in a school."

"I tried asking my teacher," I said. "But she can't have pets."

"There are lots of other teachers, though," said Levi.

"And we only need *one* teacher to want him," Allie Pink Girl said.

"Not just any teacher," Matt said. "A teacher without a snake."

"Most teachers don't even know about him," Levi said. "We have to tell them!"

I wiped my eyes with my hand. They wanted to help! "Maybe we could write a letter," I said. "And give it to all the teachers at our schools?"

"That's a great idea!" Levi said. "Operation Jelly Bean!"

When Ms. Kim came back, we told her our plan. She smiled and said, "That's wonderful! First, I have a surprise, remember? After that, let's brainstorm a letter. When we're done, I'll make copies for you all to take to school."

Ms. Kim's special surprise was five black puppies! "Their names are Charlie, Casey, Checkers, Clover, and Cody," she said.

We all squealed when we saw them. "And this time you can go inside the cages with them," Ms. Kim said.

We each had one puppy to play with. Ms. Kim had dog toys and a whole stack of picture books for us to read to our puppy. "They won't understand the story," Ms. Kim said. "But they'll love hearing your voice and being close with you."

My puppy's name was Charlie. He tried to chew the pages of *Go, Dog. Go!* He also chewed the toys, my pants legs, and his bed. He even chewed my hair when I picked him up. But I didn't mind. Along with the chewing came lots of happy wiggling and tail wagging and licky kisses.

When Ms. Kim told us it was time for us to go, Jada said, "It's so hard to leave them!"

"They probably won't be here very long,"
Ms. Kim said. "Lots of people come into the
shelter hoping for a puppy. Do you still want to
write a letter about Jelly Bean? We'll have
to hurry to get it done before your parents
get here."

As we left the kennel, the puppies put their paws up against the sides of their cages. They gave little yappy barks and wagged their tails.

It was really hard to go, but I was excited, too. In Ms. Kim's office, we crowded around her computer. "Operation Jelly Bean gets under way!" Matt said.

"Do you want me to type the letter?" Levi asked.

I felt warm with happiness. I didn't have to find Jelly Bean a home by myself anymore — we were doing this together. "Let's put a photo of Jelly Bean in the letter," I said.

"Good idea!" Jada said. "His cuteness is hard to resist!"

"We have some great photos of him on our website," Ms. Kim said. "We can put one at the bottom of the letter."

Levi sat down at the computer. "We need a catchy opening for the letter. Maybe something funny to get the teachers' attention." He started typing.

Dear Teachers,

A new student wants to join your class! He's smart and sweet and doesn't even need a desk! The Maplewood Animal Shelter has a wonderful guinea pig named Jelly Bean who needs a home. We think Jelly Bean would make a great pet for a classroom. Maybe yours!

"Let's say why he'd be a good pet for a class," Jada added.

"He likes to be petted," I said. "And he wants to be in the middle of the action."

He's friendly, likes to be petted and held, and is happy in the middle of lots of activity. He doesn't bite anything — except carrots!

"We should tell them how much he costs," Allie Pink Girl said. "So they'll see he's not too expensive."

"And they can get the cage for ten dollars," Matt added. "Because a new cage costs a lot more than that."

He costs $20.

"Put *only costs*," Jada said. "And an exclamation point."

He only costs $20! For $10 more, you can
get his cage, water bottle, food dishes,
and little wooden hidey house, too.
What a deal!

"That sounds good," Jada said.

"Can we say he's educational?" Matt asked.
"Teachers like that."

"And pets teach responsibility," added
Ms. Kim.

Having a pet is fun and educational. It helps teach responsibility!

Come in TODAY and get him. Just imagine how excited your students will be and how happy Jelly Bean will be to have a home at last — with you.

Sincerely,

The Shelter Pet Squad

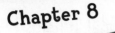

Chapter 8

Second Chances Can Take a While

"Can I put one of these letters into every teacher's mailbox?" I asked Mr. Lightfoot, our school secretary, on Monday morning.

"What's your letter about?" he asked.

"A guinea pig," I said.

"Let me see." Mr. Lightfoot held out his hand, so I gave him a copy. He smiled as he read it. "My children had a guinea pig when they were little."

"Would they like *another* one?" I asked quickly.

He laughed, handing me back my letter. "No. My children are grown-ups now. But good luck! I hope you find Jelly Bean a new family."

"Me, too," I said.

Mr. Lightfoot gave me a step stool so I could reach the mailboxes on the top row. I put one letter in every box.

With each one, I made a wish. *Find Jelly Bean a home.*

All week, I waited for Saturday to come. I imagined the shelter opening and a line of teachers waiting at the door. They would be pushing and shoving to be first inside to adopt Jelly Bean. If more than one teacher wanted him, maybe the shelter would have to draw names!

When I arrived at the shelter on Saturday, I felt excited but also a little sad that Jelly Bean wouldn't be there. "Hi," I said to Ms. Flores, and hurried to the small-animal room. Maybe there were some new small pets?

When I stepped inside, Jelly Bean stood up on his hind legs. *"Wheeek!"* My heart hurt. I hadn't brought him a carrot or an apple or anything. I had been so sure he'd be gone.

"You can give him some timothy hay," Ms. Flores said behind me. "There's some in the bag under his cage."

Jelly Bean made happy little guinea pig chuckles as I put a handful of hay in his dish. I wanted to cry.

"Suzannah, be sure you close the door when you leave," Ms. Flores said. "We need to keep the door to the small-animal room closed now."

"Why? Jelly Bean likes people," I said.

"Yes, but he doesn't like cats," Ms. Flores said. "We've discovered that Jelly Bean gets very upset if Hattie or Shadow comes in there.

He didn't seem to mind the cats when he first came, but the longer he's with us, the less happy he seems to be."

"But he'll be sad in here all by himself," I said.

"I know. But Hattie and Shadow need to be in the waiting room. They do such a good job greeting our visitors. To be honest, I've been thinking that maybe a different shelter could find Jelly Bean a home faster. Or maybe they'd have other guinea pigs to keep him company. I sent an email to some other shelters, asking if one of them can take him."

"Oh, please don't do that!" I had promised that *I'd* find him a home. If he went to another shelter, I might never know what happened to him.

"We have to do what's best for him, Suzannah," she said.

When I got to the workroom for Shelter Pet Squad, I felt as low as a worm underground. "I can't believe Jelly Bean is still here."

"We all tried," Levi said. "I guess no one is looking for a guinea pig right now."

"Did anyone come to *look* at Jelly Bean?" Jada asked Ms. Kim.

She shook her head. "I'm sorry. We can't always make things work out as quickly as we'd like. So when it finally *does* happen, it's something to celebrate. Wonderful families came in this week. All five puppies were adopted."

"Wow! That was fast!" Matt said.

"Bella and Sweetie also went to new homes

this week," Ms. Kim said. "Bella had been at the shelter a long time. She had to wait months and months for her second chance, but it finally happened. All of our animals deserve a second chance, and sometimes it takes a while to come."

There was a pile of empty plastic juice bottles on the worktable, along with some dog kibble. We put a handful of kibble in each empty bottle to make fun, new toys for the dogs.

"We'll leave the caps off the bottles," Ms. Kim said. "As the dog rolls the bottle around, kibble will fall out, giving treats. We need to be careful with plastic, but these juice bottles are tough. They won't crack when the dogs bite them."

In the kennel, it was fun watching the dogs play. They chased the bottles all over their pens. They worked hard to get the kibble out. I couldn't feel happy, though. I hadn't kept my promise. I hadn't found Jelly Bean a home. And maybe now he'd be going to another shelter.

After we'd visited the dogs, the other kids went to play with the cats. But I asked Ms. Kim if I could visit Jelly Bean.

"Of course," she said.

In the waiting room, I asked Ms. Flores if I could give him another treat. "Let's see if he's eaten all his hay," she said. When we opened the door to the small-animal room, Jelly Bean stood up on his hind legs. *"Wheeek!"*

But then he clacked his teeth together. He

darted into his wooden hidey house. All I could see was the side of his face in the doorway. "What's the matter with him?" I asked.

"Oh, Hattie, get out of here!" Ms. Flores said, shooing the cat out of the room. "I didn't notice she'd snuck in with us."

After Hattie was gone, Jelly Bean still

didn't come out of his hidey house. I reached into my pocket. I didn't really need to bring Whiskers anymore, but I liked having him with me.

"Ms. Flores, may I leave my mouse here to watch over Jelly Bean?" I asked. "He always makes me feel better."

"Are you sure you want to leave him for a whole week?" she asked.

I nodded.

"All right," she said.

I sat Whiskers on the windowsill near Jelly Bean's cage. My pocket felt empty, but I liked seeing Whiskers's brave smile. When I turned around, Jelly Bean was munching and crunching his hay.

"He seems much happier now," Ms. Flores said.

I smiled. Maybe Whiskers's bravery was catching, like the sneezy flu.

The bell over the front door rang. "I'll be right back," Ms. Flores said. As the door to the small-animal room closed, I whispered to Jelly

Bean, "I tried everything I could think of to get you a home. I don't know what else to do."

I wondered if the girl who had to give up Jelly Bean still missed him. Or if she thought he'd already found a new home by now.

From the waiting room, I heard Ms. Flores yell, "Shelter Pet Squad, come quick!"

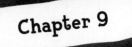

Chapter 9

Jelly Bean's Second Chance

Ms. Flores was smiling at a lady standing at the counter. Between them was our letter about Jelly Bean.

"Ms. Taylor, the kids can answer your questions," Ms. Flores said. "This is our Shelter Pet Squad. They wrote the letter about Jelly Bean."

"Hello," the lady said. "I loved your letter. I was wondering if Jelly Bean is still here?"

"Yes, he is!" I said. "He's in the small-animal room! Do you want to meet him?"

"But wait! First we need to know something," Matt said. "Do you have a snake?"

Ms. Taylor looked surprised. "A snake? No. I have a kindergarten class. I think my students would love to have Jelly Bean join our room."

I grinned. Just what we hoped!

"Hooray!" Jada said. "He'll like being in a classroom full of kids."

"The letter says I can buy his cage and water bottle and dishes, too?" Ms. Taylor asked. "I thought he might feel more comfortable if some things stayed the same."

I grinned. I liked that she cared if Jelly Bean felt at home.

"Yes," Ms. Flores said. "We're glad to send you home with everything he came with."

"He loves attention," Levi said. "And carrots."

"My students will give him lots of attention," Ms. Taylor said. "And I like carrots, too. So that won't be a problem."

"Be careful not to hang your kids' art projects near his cage," Matt said. "He likes to chew things."

She laughed. "I'll remember that."

"Have you thought about school vacations?" Ms. Flores said. "He'll need a place to go when school is closed."

"He can come home with me during vacations and in the summer," Ms. Taylor said. "I'd like having his company."

"Do you have a cat?" I asked. "He gets scared by cats."

"I don't have any other pets," Ms. Taylor said. "So I can give him plenty of attention."

"I think this sounds perfect for Jelly Bean,"

Ms. Flores said. "Shelter Pet Squad, what do you think?"

We all agreed.

I was sure that Jelly Bean's first family would have thought so, too.

Ms. Flores explained the paperwork. Ms. Taylor signed it and paid the adoption fee.

"We'll help you carry everything to the car," Ms. Kim said.

Jada picked up Jelly Bean's hay.

"I'll get his food," said Allie Pink Girl.

"Matt and I can carry the cage," Levi said.

While everyone was busy, I took Whiskers off the windowsill and put him back in my pocket. Now I might need some help being brave.

"The cage is a bit heavy," Ms. Flores said. "We don't want Jelly Bean to get bounced around. Let's carry him." She took him out of his cage.

"Can I carry him?" I asked.

I had never held a guinea pig before, so Ms. Flores showed me how. "Cup one hand here under his back feet, so he feels safe," she said. "And then hold him snugly against your chest. Ready?"

I nodded. Jelly Bean nuzzled my shoulder as I carried him to Ms. Taylor's car. "It's going to be okay," I whispered toward his tiny ear. "Ms. Taylor is a good match for you. You'll have kids to play with and plenty of treats. And

if you ever feel scared, you can go into your hidey house."

Levi and Matt set up the big cage on the backseat of Ms. Taylor's car. Allie Pink Girl put the guinea pig food on the floor. Jada added the hay. Ms. Taylor put her copy of the adoption papers on the front seat.

Everyone was waiting for me to put Jelly Bean in his cage. They were waiting for Ms. Taylor to take him away to his new life in kindergarten.

I stroked him behind his ears. "Good-bye, Jelly Bean." I placed him carefully inside his cage on the backseat. "I'll miss you a lot."

"Thank you all so much," Ms. Taylor said. "I'll take good care of him. I promise."

Ms. Flores, Ms. Kim, and the whole Shelter Pet Squad stayed at the edge of the parking lot. We waved until Ms. Taylor's car drove out of sight.

I blinked back tears, a little sad and a little happy. "When animals are adopted, I always feel a little bit sorry to see them go," Ms. Flores said. "Only for a moment, though. Then I'm happy that the pet has a home of his own with someone to love him."

"Jelly Bean will have lots of someones to love him," Jada said.

"A whole entire kindergarten class!" Allie Pink Girl said.

I couldn't talk. Ms. Kim put her arm around my shoulders.

I hoped Jelly Bean would be brave and Ms. Taylor would love him as much as we did. He had what Ms. Kim said every shelter pet wanted.

He got his second chance.

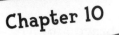

Chapter 10

Happy Endings

All week, I imagined Jelly Bean in his kinder-garten class. The kids would be so happy to see him that maybe they'd squeal or clap with joy or all want to hold him. It might scare him at first.

But Ms. Taylor seemed like a nice person who cared a lot about Jelly Bean. She'd make it okay. And I knew the kids would learn how to make him happy.

He'd poke his head out of his hidey house during math.

During reading, he'd peek at the kids from his cage.

And at lunchtime?

He'd be up on his hind legs, checking to see if anyone had carrot sticks. I hoped Ms. Taylor would remember to bring him one.

On Saturday, it felt strange to go to the shelter. Jelly Bean wouldn't be there. We had apples at home, but I had no pet to bring one for.

That feeling lasted only until Mom drove into the parking lot, though. I had helped Jelly Bean find his new home, but there were other animals at the shelter. They needed things to play with. They needed people to care about them while they waited for their second chance, too.

By the time I walked through the door for Shelter Pet Squad, I was ready. Ready for a new adventure and a new mission. Maybe there would be puppies to read to. Or dogs that needed toys. Or cats that needed petting. As Ms. Kim said, those are little things we can do for the animals, but little things matter.

"Suzannah, we've been waiting for you," Ms. Kim said. "Come see the bulletin board!"

And there was a surprise so wonderful that I laughed out loud.

I saw Jelly Bean's happy ending.

Fast Facts About Guinea Pigs

- A guinea pig is also called a cavy.
- Male guinea pigs are boars. Females are sows. Babies are pups.
- Guinea pigs are rodents. They aren't related to pigs at all!
- Guinea pigs usually live five to seven years.
- They are originally from South America.
- When they're happy, guinea pigs make a soft purring sound. They can also squeak (*wheeek!*) and chuff.
- Guinea pigs are not good climbers or jumpers, but they can hop a few inches into the air when they're excited. That's called "popcorning"! They look like popcorn popping.
- Guinea pigs' teeth grow all the time. They must gnaw hay, wood, and other firm things to wear them down.

• Many rodents are nocturnal (awake at night, asleep during the day), but not guinea pigs. They take small naps, but they are awake for most of the day.
• Guinea pigs have no tails.
• Guinea pigs are social animals. Most like the company of other guinea pigs and people.

You can learn more about guinea pigs
at the library and online.

Ways YOU Can Help Shelter Animals in Your Area

• Volunteer! Ask if your local shelter has programs for kids. The shelter might have age rules about working directly with the animals, but there are other important jobs, too, like making signs and posters or mixing up treats.

• Donate needed supplies. Animal shelters always need donations: old towels, sheets, blankets, pet toys and food, kitty litter, and office supplies. Many shelters have a "wish list" on their websites.

> • Maybe you or your friends have pet equipment at home that you aren't using.

> • Gather up any unwanted tennis balls or small stuffed animals and donate them to your shelter for dog toys. Before you bring stuffed animals to

the shelter, check them over carefully and remove any parts that the dog might swallow (such as plastic eyes or batteries). If you can't remove those parts, it's not a good toy to donate. If you're not sure, you can show the toys to the people at the shelter and let them decide.

• You could even hold a donation drive to collect things the shelter needs. Ask if you can place a donation box and a list of items to donate at school where everyone will see it. Then bring those donations to the shelter.

• Many shelters have someone who will visit classrooms and clubs to talk about their work and the animals they serve. Most shelters also offer tours of the shelter. You can suggest these ideas to your teacher or club leader.

• Interview someone from your local shelter for your school newspaper.

• Create a poster featuring adoptable animals at your shelter. Be sure to ask permission before you hang your poster at school or in your community.

• Participate in your local events. Shelters often hold walkathons, contests, bake sales, pet shows, and more.

• At your next birthday party, ask guests to bring a donation for a shelter (dog food, kitty litter, toys, or other pet items) instead of presents.

• Read about animals so you can make good decisions for your pets and for animals everywhere.

Paper-Tube Treat Puzzles

To make the dog treat puzzles that Suzannah makes in the story, you will need:

- *An empty cardboard toilet-paper tube or a paper-towel tube cut in half*
- *Small treats for dogs, such as: cheese cubes, broken-up dog biscuits, pieces of hot dog*

1. Pinch one end of the tube. Fold over the edge about half an inch to close the bottom of the tube. Fold it firmly so nothing will fall out of the tube.

2. Hold the tube with the open end up, like it's a cup. Put treats in the tube. Don't fill it all the way to the top.

3. Pinch the open end of the tube. Fold over the top edge about half an inch, sealing the treats inside. If you can't fold over the top, remove a few treats and try again.

4. Give it to a dog and watch him have fun! When he's done, be sure to clean up the ripped bits of paper tube.

Braided Fleece Toys

To make the braided fleece cat toys that Suzannah makes in the story, you will need:

- *Fleece fabric in different colors*
- *Safety scissors*
- *Measuring tape*

1. Cut your fleece into strips 3 inches wide and 40 inches long.

2. Choose three different colored strips and lay the strips one on top of the other.

3. Knot the three strips together by tying a knot a few inches from the top of the strips.

4. Braid the three strips, stopping a few inches from the bottom.

How to Braid

After you've tied the top knot, spread out the three strips. You will have a left strip, a middle strip, and a right strip. The different color strips will change their positions as you braid, but you will always have one strip on the left, one in the middle, and one on the right.

• Pick up the left strip. Cross it over the middle strip. Pull them tightly.
• Pick up the right strip. Cross it over the strip that's now in the middle. Pull tightly.
• Continue braiding left-over-middle, right-over-middle, pulling tightly.

Hint: One way to get a tight braid is to sit down and hold the top knot between your knees. That way you can hold the strips securely as you braid with your hands.

5. Stop braiding a few inches from the bottom of the strips. Tie a knot. Now you have a knot at both ends with braiding in the middle.

6. Have fun! Drag your toy along the floor for cats to pounce on, or hang it in a place where cats can swat it.

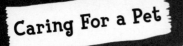

Is a Guinea Pig a Good Pet for Me?

Guinea pigs can make wonderful pets. Bringing a pet into your family is a big decision, though. Here are some questions your family should think about if you are considering a guinea pig as a pet.

• Does everyone in your family agree that a guinea pig is a good pet for you? Adding a pet is a family decision, even if the pet lives in a cage in your room.

• Do you have time for a guinea pig? Every day you will need to be sure your guinea pig has food, water, hay, and a clean cage. Guinea pigs also need daily attention from their owners and/or other guinea pigs.

• Is anyone in your family allergic to animals or timothy hay? If so, a guinea pig might not be a good pet for your family.

• Do you have money for a guinea pig? In addition to buying the guinea pig or paying the adoption fee, you will need: a cage, water bottle, food dish, things to chew, as well as regular purchases of bedding and food. You will also need to take your guinea pig to the vet if he becomes sick.

• Can you set some good rules to keep your guinea pig safe? Always hold him securely. Be gentle, kind, and calm with him. Guinea pigs can be hurt if they are squeezed or dropped. Some are frightened by loud noises and sudden movements. A guinea pig that doesn't feel safe might bite. So be sure to have rules about who can hold him and how to keep him safe.

• Should you adopt two or one? If you can adopt a pair of guinea pigs that live together, they will have each other's company when you are not there. If you adopt a single guinea pig, he will need more attention from you.

• To learn more, there are many good books and websites about guinea pigs. Knowing as much as you can about guinea pigs will help you decide if they will be a good pet for your family.

Meet My Shelter Pet

A real guinea pig inspired this book. One day I received a newsletter from my local animal shelter. Inside there was a photograph of an adorable guinea pig. His name was Cookies and Cream, and he needed a new home.

Something about that guinea pig touched my heart. I kept looking at his photo and thinking about him. So we adopted him. Cookies and Cream was a long name to say, so we just call him Cookie.

At the shelter, one of the workers helped me carry his cage to my car. She told me that his first family had children. They had cried giving him up. That's all I know about them. If I could talk to those children, I would tell them that Cookie is very loved at my house. His cage is in my living room (where he can *wheek* at anyone who walks by to bring him a treat! Lettuce and carrots are his favorites).

Now I volunteer at my local animal shelter. I love taking care of the animals and making things for them. I'm always excited when they find new families. Every animal has a story when they arrive at the shelter and another story begins when they leave us. That's really where the idea for the Shelter Pet Squad series came from.

Right now I have four pets at my house: a

dog named Milo, two bunnies (Blueberry and Muffin), and Cookie, the guinea pig. You can learn more about me and see more photos of my pets at my website: www.cynthialord.com.

– Cynthia Lord

Cookie